CODEMASTER

BOOK #1

How to Write and Decode Secret Messages

CODEMASTER

BOOK #1

How to Write and Decode Secret Messages

by Marvin Miller

Scholastic Inc.
New York Toronto London Auckland Sydney

ISBN 0-590-37386-2

These codes were previously published in *Boys' Life* magazine.

12 11 10 9 8 7 6 5 4 3 2 1 9 8/9 1 2 3/0

Printed in the U.S.A. 40
First Scholastic printing, January 1998

For

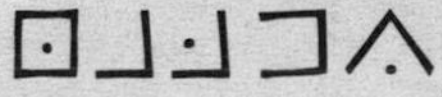, 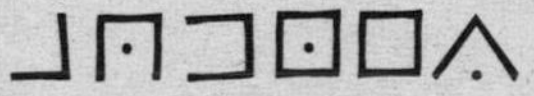, and 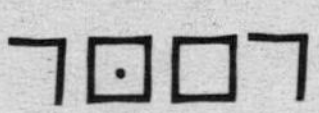

Contents

CODEMASTER

BOOK #1

How to Write and Decode
Secret Messages

Introduction

Would you like to send your best friend a message without anyone else knowing what it says? If you think it would be fun, then close the door, pull down the shades, and discover the secret world of codes!

Codes have lots of different uses. You can use them to pass notes in school or write down your innermost feelings in a diary. They all are kept perfectly safe from a nosy little brother or a tattletale big sister.

If you and your friends have a club, codes are a neat way to exchange messages and passwords. They are sure to outfox even the brainiest spy.

Bound into this book is a special bonus—a real code machine. A version of it actually was used during the American Civil War (1861–1865). Cut it out and use it to send secret messages.

Coded writing has been used for thousands of

years. Generals planning surprise attacks used it. Spies, secret agents, and smugglers all used it. Famous people used it. Even Franklin Delano Roosevelt, before he became president, wrote his secret diaries in code.

Most of the time when people talk about codes they really mean ciphers. Ciphers are a special kind of secret writing in which the words and letters have been shuffled, twisted, or disguised in all sorts of ways. In this book, the word *code* is used to mean *cipher*.

Before you turn the page, here is a word of warning. Be sure to hide this code book in a *very* safe place. Only you and your special friends should know its secrets. After all, you wouldn't want a curious spy snoop to discover it!

Are you ready? Then turn the page and begin.

Happy coding!

The Pinhole Code

Careful! You are being followed by a snoopy spy. He suspects that you plan to drop off a secret message.

He follows your every move as you casually walk along reading a magazine. Then you slow down, toss the magazine into a trash can, and move on. The spy thinks he has discovered your secret. He pulls out the magazine and carefully studies each page.

Nothing. No code or secret writing. Just a plain old magazine. Disappointed, he throws it back into the trash and hurries to catch up to you.

Guess what. The spy doesn't realize that your secret message was left behind! It is hidden in the magazine ready for your friend to find.

How did you fool the spy? You did it without even writing down a word. You just used the pinhole code.

All you need to make a pinhole code is a magazine or newspaper and a safety pin. That's it.

The pinhole code was invented in England almost 200 years ago when it was expensive to send a letter, but newspapers could be mailed for free. People who could not afford to mail a letter figured out a clever way to write to their friends. They would make pin-prick holes above printed letters in the newspaper until they spelled out a message. It didn't cost a cent to send.

And that is the secret of the pinhole code.

Suppose you want to send the message **DANGER** in pinhole code.

Begin at the top of any magazine article. Just look for the first word that contains the letter **D** (or **d**) and make a pinhole above the letter. Then look for the next letter **A** (or **a**). Continue poking holes above each letter until the entire word is "pinholed."

Now you know how it works. But how does your friend know on which page of the magazine to find your message?

Very easy! In the lower right-hand corner of the first page, you make pinholes to tell him the page number. Six holes means he will find your message on page 6.

After making the coded message, you can leave the magazine in plain view. It can be dropped on top of a pile of magazines, left on a table, tucked in a mailbox, or put anywhere you and your friend decide. When your friend opens the magazine, he holds the page up to the light. That makes it easier to see the holes.

MYSTERY BOOK

Before you try your own pinhole code message, go back to the beginning of this chapter. Do you notice the tiny dots above certain letters? Surprise! The first two paragraphs have been coded. The dots stand for pinholes. They spell out the title of a favorite book. BUT . . . there is a trick. The dot was placed above the letter that is *next to* the one you need to solve the code. So to figure out the title of the book, write down the letter to the left of the one with the dot/pinhole.

Now that you can "see through" the pinhole code, it's your turn. Grab an old magazine and create a secret message of your own.

Homer Price, written by Robert McCloskey, is the mystery book.

THE UNDERCOVER POSTCARD

Did you know that you can send a secret message on a postcard? It's handy to use whenever you go on vacation.

First write a newsy note on the card, telling your friend all about the fun you are having. But you can add a secret message. And no one but your friend knows where to find it.

Where? Under the stamp, of course!

Write a short message in pencil in tiny letters on the top right-hand corner of the card. Then paste a stamp on top of it. Make sure to use a gummed stamp. A self-adhesive stamp won't work as well.

When your friend receives your postcard, she tears off the corner that has the stamp. Then she floats it in a glass of water.

The water loosens the glue. Soon she will be able to peel off the stamp. And there is your hidden message!

The Wheel Code

Shhh! Close the door and pull down the shades. Make sure no one is watching. You are about to discover a special Codemaster secret.

Get ready to learn how to construct your own decoder, bound into this book. You can use it for sending top-secret messages.

The decoder wheel was invented in the fifteenth century by the Italian architect and code expert Leon Battista Alberti. It was the first code machine ever invented and has been in use throughout the world in different forms since then. Decoder wheels made out of brass were used during the American Civil War.

The decoder wheel is made up of two disks, one inside the other, as shown on the next page. The outside disk has the alphabet in clockwise order from A to Z. The smaller inner disk looks like a hodgepodge.

It has all the letters of the alphabet, but they are all jumbled up.

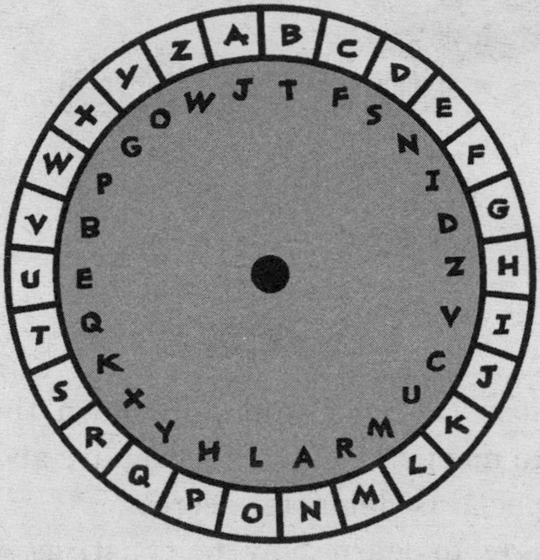

To make your own decoder wheel, cut out the two disks printed on the insert. Next, lay the smaller disk on top of the larger disk. Push a thumbtack through the center of the two pieces and tack them to a small piece of plywood.

There! You now have a genuine decoder wheel. By turning the inner disk, its letters line up with any one of the letters on the outer disk.

To use the decoder wheel to write a message, first think of any letter. Suppose you choose **H**. This is called your *key letter*. Turn the inner wheel around so the **H** lines up with the letter **A** on the outside disk. Your coder will look like this:

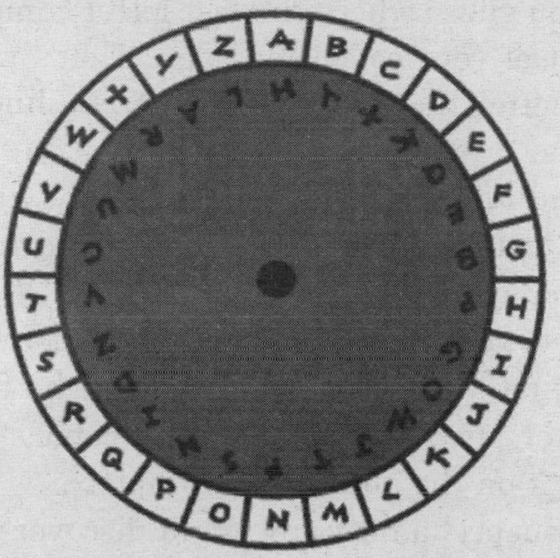

Keep the wheel in this position and you are ready to code this message:

LOCK ALL DOORS

The first letter of the message is **L**. Search for that letter on the outside disk and write down the letter that is opposite it on the inner disk. So **L** is coded as **J**.

Get the idea? Now you are ready to scramble the entire message by searching the outside disk and writing down the letters from the inside disk instead.

Your message in code will look like this:

JSXW HJJ KSSDZH

Can you guess where the last letter came from? It isn't part of your coded message. That's right! It is the key letter that you used when you lined up the two disks.

To read the message, your friend will need a decoder just like yours. You can make one out of cardboard using yours as a pattern. When your friend gets your message, she looks at the last letter and lines up the disks **H** to **A**. Then she finds each code letter on the *inner* disk and copies the letter opposite it on the outer disk. Simple!

If you suspect a nosy spy might discover your message, you can make the code even more difficult to crack. To throw off the spy, write the message backward and use different spacing between words:

HZD SSKJ JHW XSJ

A neat thing about the wheel code is that any letter can be coded 26 different ways simply by choosing a different key letter. If your key letter was **X**, the same message (written backward) would read:

XCVII EFFX TQIF

Now that you know how to use the wheel code, get started on writing your own secret messages. Don't worry if a clever spy might be watching. He will be spinning around in circles trying to figure them out!

Use your coder to figure out the title of this book. (Careful, it is coded backward.)

FQDKJGPX NTSKQ QDEH

If you came up with *Freedom's Children* by Ellen Levine, you have just mastered the wheel code.

The Playing Card Code

Imagine this: A spy sneaks into your code club headquarters and searches for a secret message. All he finds are some books, games, a soccer ball, and a pile of playing cards on a table.

He can't find the message anywhere. But it was right under his nose. He never realized that the playing cards were really a message in disguise.

You fooled him with the playing card code.

This is how it works:

You start by pulling two full suits of cards from a deck. Let's say you choose diamonds and clubs. There are 13 cards in each suit for a total of 26 cards. Can you figure out why 26 cards would be helpful for sending a secret message?

Simple! There are 26 letters in the alphabet. So each card can stand for a different letter.

Here are the letters:

DIAMONDS	CLUBS
Ace = A	**Ace = N**
2 = B	**2 = O**
3 = C	**3 = P**
4 = D	**4 = Q**
5 = E	**5 = R**
6 = F	**6 = S**
7 = G	**7 = T**
8 = H	**8 = U**
9 = I	**9 = V**
10 = J	**10 = W**
Jack = K	**Jack = X**
Queen = L	**Queen = Y**
King = M	**King = Z**

This is the key to the code. The sender needs to know it in order to encode his message, and the receiver needs to know the key in order to decipher the code.

But what do you do if your secret message contains the same letter a second time? If this happens, use one of the hearts or spades cards to repeat the letter. For example, the letter **F** can be either the six of diamonds or the six or hearts (both are red cards). Likewise, the letter **S** can be either the six of clubs or the six of spades (both are black cards).

If your message has the same letter repeated

more than twice, you'll need an extra deck of cards to complete the code.

Suppose you want to send this message using the playing card code:

BRING THE PLANS

Spread out the cards like this:

Once the cards are all spread out, pick them up from left to right and stack them facedown in a pile. Next, turn the pile faceup so the two of diamonds is showing. The bottom card should be the six of clubs.

Leave the pile on the table, faceup. It looks innocent enough. No one would suspect that the cards spell out a hidden message.

When a code club friend picks up the pile, all she has to do is deal the cards onto the table faceup from left to right. She writes down the letter each card represents. Then she breaks the letters into words. Out pops your undercover message!

There is another slick thing about the playing card code. You can use an extra card from the pack as a “signature” card. It will tell the code reader who sent the message. You might be the jack of hearts. Someone else might choose the four of spades. Slip your signature card faceup on the bottom of the pile. If the last card is the jack of hearts, your friend knows the message is from you.

Now that you know how the playing card code works, use it to send your next secret message to a friend. Another cool thing about this code is that it’s easy to erase the evidence. All your friend has to do is shuffle the cards!

OK. Ready to try out the playing card code? See if you can unravel the title of this book:

If you had fun figuring out the code, you will have even more fun reading this book.

You have just decoded *Call It Courage*, written by Armstrong Sperry.

THE NAVAJO CODE

You want to send messages by radio but the enemy knows your code. What can you do?

Soldiers in World War II faced that problem—until someone came up with a clever idea. A number of Navajo Indians were recruited. Some worked with units that sent messages and others with units that received them.

The Indians then communicated in a code based on their native tongue. The enemy had never heard the Navajo language before. And it turned out to be an unbreakable code!

The Inside-Out Code

All right, code busters, get ready to stretch your brain muscles.

Here is a message for you to decode. Study it carefully.

GNIPMAC GNIOG MA I

Did you figure it out? The message is written backward. It says **I AM GOING CAMPING**.

Backward writing is an easy code to crack, even for a beginning spy.

Here is the same message. But the letters have been rearranged:

GNCIAOM GPMIA NI G

Now the code looks harder. This jumbled message was written in the inside-out code. That's right. The words have been written inside out.

While it may appear difficult, making an inside-out code is easy. First, find the middle letter. **I AM GOING CAMPING** has 15 letters. The center letter is the **G**. Make a mark above it:

I AM GOING CAMPING

Then print this letter on a blank sheet of paper:

G

Next to it print the letters that are to the left and right of the **G**:

GNC

As you copy each letter, cross out the one on your original sentence. Then keep adding the remaining letters in a row, using alternate letters from the left and right of the original message:

GNCIAOMGPMIANIG

To really baffle a nosy spy, use different spacing

between groups of letters. You wind up with the inside-out coded message below:

GNCIAOM GPMIA NI G

Now get set for some practice. See how quickly you can code the message **PIZZA FOR LUNCH**. Ready? Begin!

Congratulate yourself if your message looks like this:

OFRALZUZNICPH

When your friend receives your code, he simply repeats your steps, but in backward order.

He copies down the first letter in the center of a sheet of paper.

O

Then he writes down the next two letters in the message, printing one on each side of the **O**.

FOR

He copies the rest of the letters, printing one on the left, then one on the right.

Amazing! **PIZZA FOR LUNCH** slowly appears right before his eyes.

Tip: To use the inside-out code, your first sentence should have an odd number of letters. If you have an even number of letters, add an **X** at the end.

Inside-out messages are fun to decode. And the secret is safe. Not even English teachers think to write a sentence inside out!

MYSTERY BOOK

Suppose a friend writes to you about an interesting book he just read. He wants you to read it, too. Test your code-breaking skills on this:

PP I INHG WBEO HYTX

The book is *The Whipping Boy* by Sid Fleischman.

The Spike Code

It is almost two o'clock. In another ten minutes it will be time for gym. You open your locker and kick off your shoes. First you put on one sneaker and then the other.

But wait! A piece of paper is stuck inside the toe. You poke around and pull it out. Someone has shoved some paper inside. You unfold it and open it up. Here is what you see:

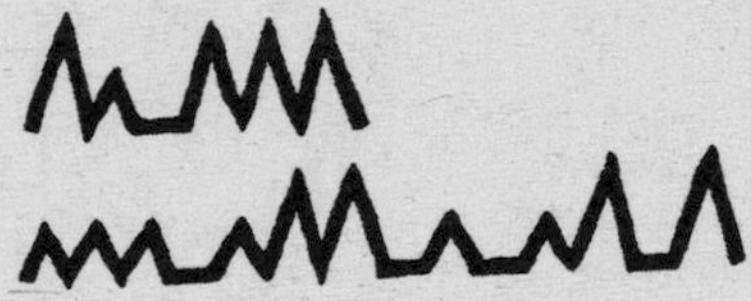

What are those peaks and valleys? Could it be a signal from outer space? A puzzled look spreads across your face.

Then suddenly you realize what you are holding. Your friend has slipped you a secret message. He has written it using the spike code. Now the strange scribbling begins to make sense. It reads:

NO SWEAT

Can you figure out how the spike code works? The secret is a cleverly disguised version of the Morse code.

Here are the dots and dashes of the Morse code:

A •—	J •———	S •••
B —•••	K —•—	T —
C —•—•	L •—••	U ••—
D —••	M ——	V •••—
E •	N —•	W •——
F ••—•	O ———	X —••—
G ——•	P •——•	Y —•——
H ••••	Q ——•—	Z ——••
I ••	R •—•	

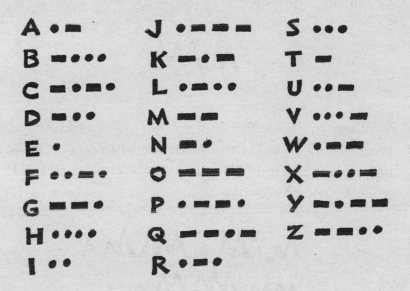

To convert the Morse code to the spike code, use a tall spike to stand for a dash and a short spike for a dot.

The letter **N** would be —• in Morse code. But when you use the spike code, it will look like this:

With all the spikes, how will your friend figure out where one letter ends and the next one begins?

You need to separate each letter by drawing a short line between the spikes. For example, the word **NO** is written —• ——— in Morse code. Using the spike code it looks like this:

When you have finished coding one word and are ready to move on to the next, simply leave a space before you continue. The message **NO ONE HOME** in spike code looks like this:

Now it's time for some practice. Encode the message **DANGER** in spike code.

Finished? Check your coded message. It should be:

A neat thing about the spike code is that it looks so mysterious. Even a spy who is a whiz at Morse code will never realize that you have used it to hide a message. He will suspect that the series of spikes is a chart of electrical waves or the sketch of a mountain range. If someone accidentally finds a copy of the Morse code in your notebook, he probably still won't figure out how it was used to make your message.

Enjoy sending secrets using the spike code. The message might look like it's from outer space. But it really is out of this world!

Now that you know the secret, test your code-cracking skills. Untangle the title of this classic book:

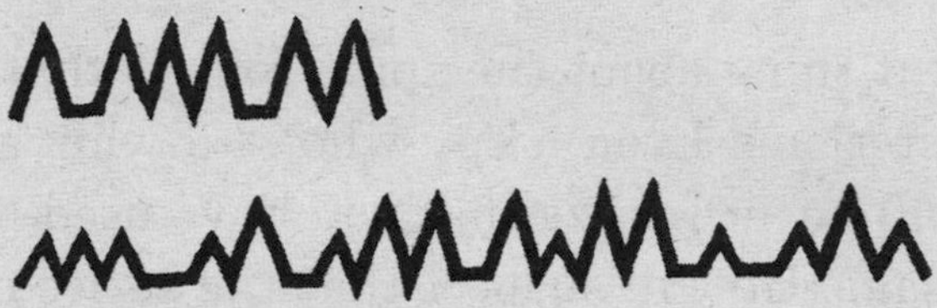

If you decoded *Tom Sawyer* by Mark Twain, you've got it right.

SECRET IN YOUR SHOE

Make a secret hiding place inside your shoe. It's perfect for carrying around secret maps, notes, or a list of your friends' phone numbers.

First, wearing socks, step on a thin piece of cardboard and trace around one of your feet. Then cut around the outline and trim the cardboard to fit inside your shoe.

Tuck whatever you want to hide into your shoe, then slip the cardboard "sole" on top. Even if you take off your shoes, your secret won't be discovered.

That's using your head . . . and your feet.

The Pigpen Code

Have you ever been to a pig farm? If you can forget about the mud and the strong odor, you might recognize this diagram:

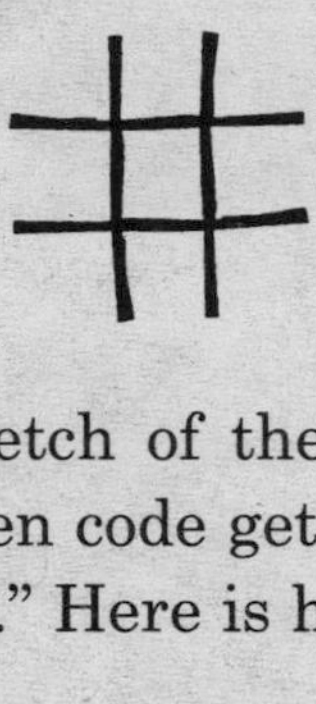

Got it? It is a sketch of the fences of a pigpen. That's how the pigpen code gets its name. Each letter has its own "pen." Here is how to begin:

Notice the box—or pen—for the letter **A**. If the box were chopped off from the rest, it would look like this:

Then remove the letter **A** and you are left with the shape of its pen:

That's right. The symbol ┘ stands for **A** in pigpen code. But wait just one second. Take a closer look at the other pigpens. No other letter has the same shaped pen. Amazing!

Move on to the next few letters. The letter **B** is ⊔ and **C** is └. **E** is in a closed box and its pigpen code is written as □.

The word **HEAD** would be coded like this:

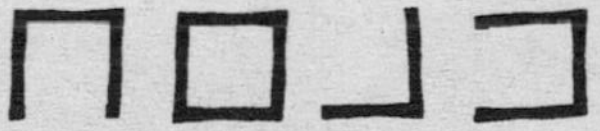

OK so far. But only nine letters fit into a pigpen. What about the rest of the alphabet?

To slip all 26 letters into different pens, you need to use another pattern, a large X. In fact, you need two pigpens and two X's. Place a dot in each compartment of the second set of diagrams:

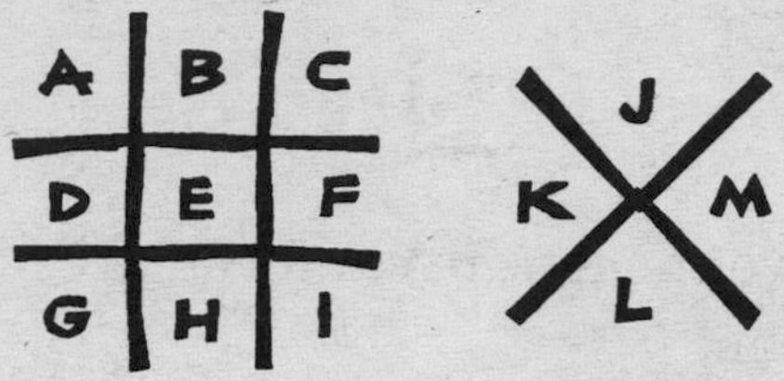

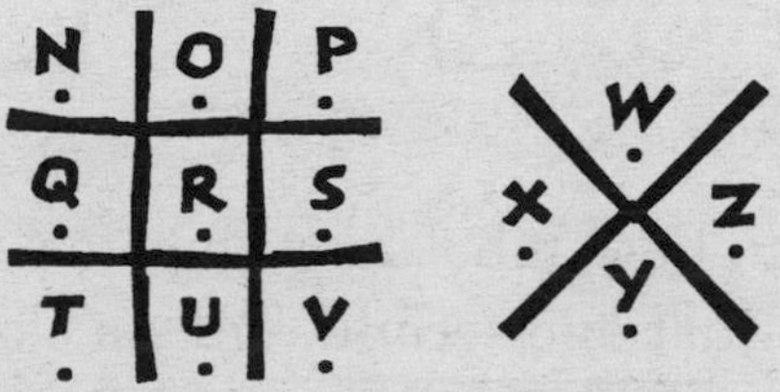

See? Now you have room for the entire alphabet! You can encode any word. Take the word **HEADLINES**:

Ready for some practice? Disguise this sentence in pigpen code:

I FINISHED MY HOMEWORK

If you did your homework correctly, your message should look like this:

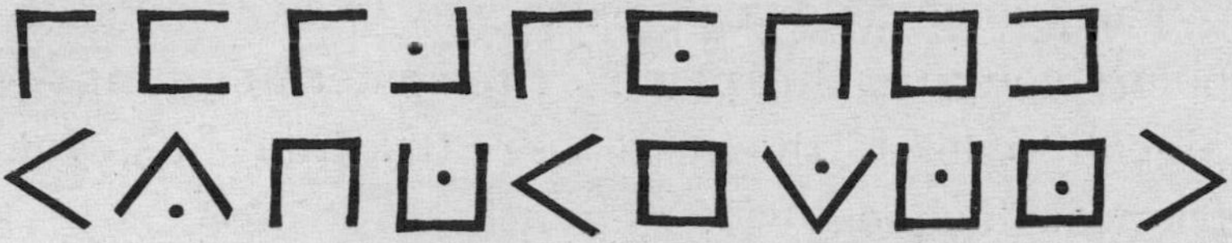

The pigpen code was actually used during the American Civil War. Confederate prisoners smuggled out messages to their fellow soldiers. If it was good enough to fool the Union guards, you can be sure it will stump a snoopy spy in your neighborhood.

If you want to be really tricky, you can make up a different pigpen code for each day of the week. Just change the order of the letters. For example, the letters inside the pens can run upward and those inside the X can be clockwise instead of counterclockwise. Here is one way to do it:

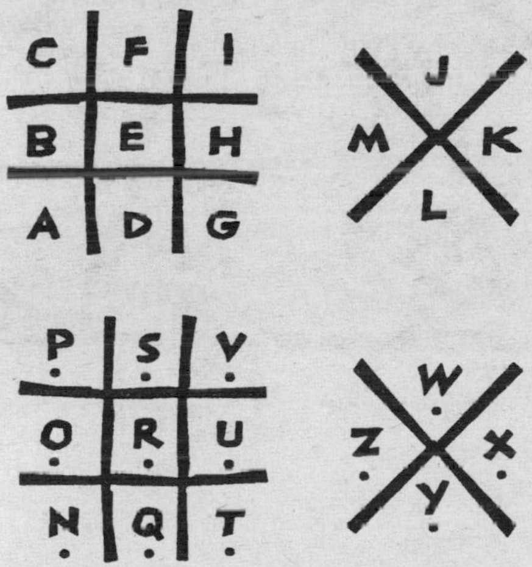

The pigpen code is a perfect way to swap jokes. So before you turn this page, write something funny in pigpen code. If the joke is really hilarious, your friend will squeal with delight!

MYSTERY BOOK

Now that you have the hang of it, use the first set of pigpens on page 30 to decode the title of this great book:

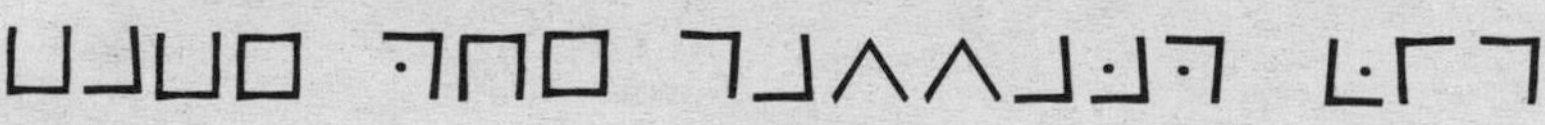

If your answer is *Babe, the Gallant Pig*, written by Dick King-Smith, let out a loud "*oink!*"

The Ruler Code

The ruler code is a speedy way to send secret messages to friends. And it offers a way to have fun with numbers.

To begin, lay a 12-inch ruler on a blank sheet of paper. Make a small dot above the 0 (the first mark on the ruler) and the 12 (the last mark). Then write a letter of the alphabet at every half-inch.

Since there are only 25 half-inch markings and 26 letters, squeeze together the Y and Z. Your sheet will look like this:

There! You have just made a secret code sheet for sending information in ruler code. By now you may have guessed the ruler code secret. The numbers on the ruler replace the letters above them.

To disguise your secret code sheet, just take away the ruler.

A B C D E F G H I J K L M N O P Q R S T U V W X Y/Z
• •

All that is left is a simple line of letters! No one will suspect that you used a ruler to make up the code. Even if someone finds your code sheet, he won't know what it means.

To write a hidden message in ruler code, position the ruler so the 0 is below one dot and the 12 is below the other. Then substitute the ruler numbers for each letter in your message.

For example, the **K** is coded as **5**, since that is the ruler number below it. The **L** is coded as **5½**. The code number **0** stands for **A** and the number **12** means **Y** or **Z**.

See how easy it is? Here is how the warning **DO NOT TRUST BARRY** looks in ruler code:

1½–7 6½–7–9½ 9½–8½–10–9–9½

½–0–8½–8½–12

When your friend gets your note, she uses her own secret code sheet that is marked the same way. Then she places her ruler below the two dots and easily unscrambles your message.

But suppose a spy finds out that you use a ruler. You can still fool him. That's one of the shrewd things about the ruler code.

What if a spy gets his hands on this coded message?

$$6\tfrac{1}{2}-12 \quad 11\tfrac{1}{2}-12-2 \quad 2-1-2\tfrac{1}{2}-1\tfrac{1}{2}-2$$

$$5\tfrac{1}{2}-5-1-1-4\tfrac{1}{2}$$

He won't be able to figure it out. When he tries to decode the numbers, all he gets is a jumble of letters. But the message is the same as the one before. It says **DO NOT TRUST BARRY**.

Can you guess how it's done?

When you want to change the ruler code, make up your secret code sheet with a different letter at the 0 mark. In this example, the first letter is **P**. This is called a key letter.

Then write out all the alphabet letters again like this:

How does your friend know your key letter? You tell her by writing it in the lower right-hand corner of your coded message. If you write down **P**, that's all the information your friend needs to make up a new secret code sheet.

Are you ready to try your hand (I mean your foot ruler) at solving a message in ruler code?

First, make up a new secret code sheet. This time, for the key letter use **X**. Now try to figure out the title of this famous book:

$$4 - 3 - 7\tfrac{1}{2} - 10\tfrac{1}{2} - 6\tfrac{1}{2} - 3 \quad 1\tfrac{1}{2} - 3 - 7\tfrac{1}{2}$$

The answer is *Gentle Ben* by Walt Morey. Congratulations! You have just decoded the secret . . . inch by inch.

THE SPACED-OUT MESSAGE

Messages—even uncoded ones—must be written carefully. Otherwise, the results can be embarrassing.

One day a man sent his friend a telegram to tell him he had tickets for a sold-out play. But the telegraph operator mistakenly added an extra space in the message.

His friend read the telegram with glee: **HAVE GOT TEN TICKETS.**

Immediately, he invited eight friends to join them. But all were disappointed when they arrived at the theater. Why?

The telegraph operator had split a word. The message was supposed to read: **HAVE GOTTEN TICKETS.**

Yipes!

The Keyboard Code

Does this series of letters look familiar?

Q W E R T Y U I O P
A S D F G H J K L
Z X C V B N M

You probably know the answer. They're the letters as they appear on a typewriter or computer keyboard. With a little effort, you can turn your keyboard into a real code machine.

What makes the keyboard code so much fun is that your coded message appears instantly, right before your eyes. You type in one letter and out comes another. Just like that!

Here is the secret of the keyboard code: Change the letters on the keyboard so that each row reads just like a regular alphabet. The first letter on the keyboard, the **Q**, becomes an **A**. The second letter, the **W**, becomes a **B**, and so on.

Making a keyboard code machine is easy. All you need are paper, scissors, glue, and a pen. Use a glue, such as rubber cement, that is easy to remove.

Draw 26 small circles on the paper and write a different letter of the alphabet in each. Make the circles about the same size as the keys.

Next, cut out the circles and paste the letters in alphabetical order on the keys. (Make sure you have the permission of the keyboard's owner.) Now the keyboard looks like this:

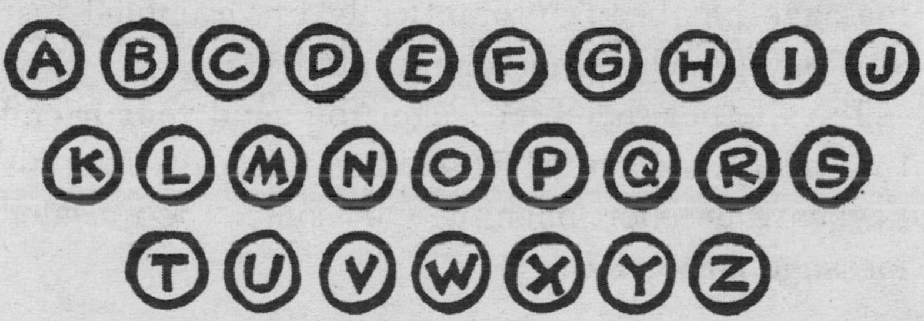

Try it out. Press the **P** key. The letter comes out as an **H**.

If you want to transform the word **HOUSE** into code, just type it in, and out comes **IGXLT**. It's that simple. Your coded message appears as fast as you can type.

To decode your message, your friend needs a keyboard code machine, too. But the letters have to be in a different order than yours. Your friend pastes letters over his keys to look like this:

When your friend types the message **IGXLT** on his decoder machine, it comes out **HOUSE**. Your message has been automatically unscrambled just as a real decoding machine would do.

Try another coded message. You send your friend the coded message **WTVQKT**. He types it into his keyboard decoder machine. Out comes the uncoded message **BEWARE**.

MYSTERY BOOK

Are you ready to try your hand—I mean your fingers—at the keyboard code? You can experiment without pasting letters over the keys. It just takes a little longer to do.

Use the decoder keyboard —the one that is not in alphabetical order.

Can you decode the title of this good book? Sit down at a keyboard and try it.

ZIT NTQKSOFU

To get you started, find the first letter, **Z**, on the keyboard. It's on the fifth key in the first row. Press that same key on your typewriter. The letter **T** appears. Now finish off the rest of the code.

When you do, you will have typed out the title of the book *The Yearling* by Marjorie Kinnan Rawlings.

The Crossword Puzzle Code

The secret to this code is an innocent-looking crossword puzzle. But as simple as it looks, the crossword puzzle code will fool even the brainiest spy.

To get started, use a ruler to draw a blank crossword grid like this:

Make another exactly like it for your friend to keep.

Now, suppose you want to send your friend the message **I AM BEING WATCHED. STAY AWAY. DO NOT CONTACT ME UNTIL MONDAY.**

First, write your message in the blank squares *from left to right*, beginning with the top left square:

In the leftover blank squares, enter any letters you wish. We used Z and K.

Next, copy the message from the crossword puzzle in code form. Here's how to do it: Starting at the top left square, copy the letters in each column, *from top to bottom*:

IIYNTUAHAONDNEWTAT
AMGDCCIBWSATLYATY
OMZETDNMOKCAOEN

When you send the coded message, write the letters again on another piece of paper, but this time, break them up into meaningless groups, like this:

IIYN TUAH AONDN EWTAT
AMG DCCI BWSATLYATY
OMZE TDNM OKC AOEN

A spy will scratch his head trying to figure out that message. But not your friend. When your message arrives, he copies the letters in the blank squares on his copy of the crossword grid, starting with the top left blank and continuing from top to bottom. It will look just like the crossword puzzle you made.

Your friend now reads the crossword message from left to right, and your words become unscrambled.

If you like this code, you may want to run off lots of copies of this grid on a copy machine. You can use a grid like this for any message that has about 50 letters. You may also want to make some smaller grids with fewer squares to use for shorter messages.

You can have hours of fun writing messages with the crossword puzzle code. And if a spy snoop tries to figure them out, you're sure to cross him up!

MYSTERY BOOK

Now that you have the hang of the crossword puzzle code, try to decode this book title:

**TIUYL ONBR SAHCLHB RRE
NUD EJEER ED YNKI OBIF**

Use the crossword grid below. It is smaller than the first one because there are fewer letters in the code. Also, the black blocks are in a different pattern, just to be tricky.

Congratulate yourself if you figured out that the title is *The Incredible Journey*, written by Sheila Burnford.

The Ice-Cream Bar Code

Delicious! You and your friend have just finished the last lick of your ice-cream bars.

But wait. Don't throw away the sticks. You can use your sticks to make identical secret code machines.

Sound interesting? Then lick your lips and read on.

Begin by making pencil marks along the top edges of your sticks. Vary the spacing between the marks:

There you have your two coding machines! You can use them to write and decode messages.

Suppose you want to encode the message **BOX CONTAINS PLANS**, to send to your friend.

Place your stick flat on a sheet of paper. Above the

first mark, print any capital letter that has a straight line on its left side (the letters B, D, E, F, H, K, L, M, N, P, and R can be used). Line up the straight line of the letter with the first mark on your stick. Then print the first word of your message, one letter above each mark:

F   B O X

Continue by writing each word on a separate line. Remember to start off with a straight-line letter first to make sure all the letters in the message line up.

Here's how your message looks now:

F B O X
H C O NT A I N S
L P L AN S

You're not finished yet! Disguise the message by adding fake letters in between the real ones:

F LSBVOWX
H TFCUOSVNTBNIASPICNQS
L ARPXLVNANWASS

Now your secret message is completely hidden in a jumble of gibberish.

When your friend receives your note, she takes out her own code stick. She lines up the mark below the beginning straight-line letter and starts her decoding. Your hidden message pops out above the stick!

Another way to make a coder like this is to use a pencil. Make the marks with a nail file and they will look like the bite marks of a "pencil nibbler."

Mystery Book

Now you can test your skills to find out how easy this code is to use. If you don't have a stick handy, trace the marks from the stick shown on page 49 on the edge of an index card.

Can you figure out the title of this book?

P L S U T PZASTMSOADJIFR L S

F Z T RNOPLOM

You have just decoded *Upstairs Room* by Johanna Reiss.

Treat yourself to an ice-cream bar.

TRICKING A BRAINY SPY

Suppose you receive a hidden message that seems a little suspicious. Was it really written by a friend? Or did an outsider figure out your code and send you a fake message instead?

Sometimes real secret agents use a "security check" so the person who receives the message will know that it is genuine.

A security check is a prearranged coding mistake that is used in all transmissions. For example, a letter in a specific position can be deliberately wrong.

Let's say that you and your partner agreed on a security check for the ninth letter. Then you received the ice-cream bar code message below. Was it really sent by your friend? Or was it a phony?

HMZBMRDAINOHNG

DVCAJON

LKDUT NSHBRCXSELZLELTJA

That's right. **UMBRELLA** is misspelled **UNBRELLA** (**N** is the ninth letter of the message). That's your signal that the coded message is real!

The Mixed-up Math Code

Do you ever get math problems wrong on purpose? Probably not.

But with the mixed-up math code, you have to be an expert at getting wrong answers.

In this code, each letter of the alphabet stands for a number:

A = 1	**B = 2**	**C = 3**	**D = 4**
E = 5	**F = 6**	**G = 7**	**H = 8**
I = 9	**J = 10**	**K = 11**	**L = 12**
M = 13	**N = 14**	**O = 15**	**P = 16**
Q = 17	**R = 18**	**S = 19**	**T = 20**
U = 21	**V = 22**	**W = 23**	**X = 24**
Y = 25	**Z = 26**		

To write the letter **E** in a secret message, you use

number **5**. Now, to write **E** in the mixed-up math code, here is what you do:

Make up a math problem and **add 5** to the correct answer. Write down this wrong answer. The math problem might look like this:

10 - 8 = 7

The correct answer is 2. So you add 5 to 2 and get 7. The person receiving your secret message simply *subtracts* the right answer (2) from the wrong answer (7) and gets 5, or the letter **E**.

Here is how to send the word **HAT**:

8 + 4 = 20
6 - 2 = 5
7 x 6 = 62

Did you work it out like this?

The right answer 12 subtracted from the wrong answer 20 is 8, or H.

The right answer 4 subtracted from the wrong answer 5 is 1, or A.

The right answer 42 subtracted from the wrong answer 62 is 20, or T.

To make the message even more secret, write it on

a piece of your old math homework. It will look just like a set of equations.

Are you ready to test your skill? Try this riddle: What is black and white and has leaves? Here is the answer in mixed-up math code:

3 + 5 = 9

16 - 11 = 7

6 + 2 = 23

4 x 3 = 27

15 ÷ 5 = 14

If you didn't get "a book" for the answer, recheck your arithmetic. Remember: Subtract each equation's correct answer from the false one.

Just a word of warning. Don't let your secret message fall into your parents' hands. You'll have a tough time explaining how you got all wrong answers!

The Compass Code

Almost everyone knows how to use a compass. But the compass code is still a big secret.

A compass helps prevent someone from getting lost. But with the compass code, the exact opposite happens. It's a neat way to trick a pesky spy. You will confuse him . . . and then you'll lose him.

To make a compass code, begin with the points of a compass:

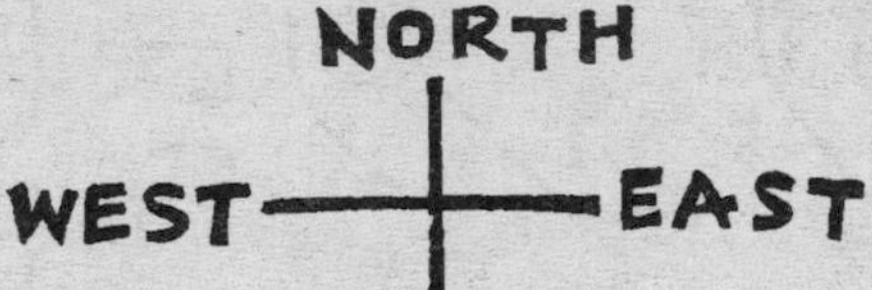

Next, write the first four letters of the alphabet, one next to each line, moving clockwise.

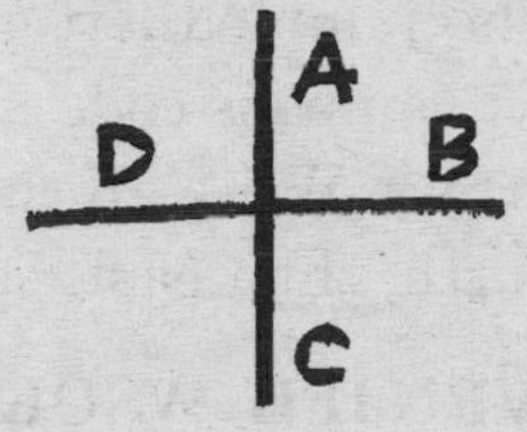

Add more letters in alphabetical order, until it looks like this:

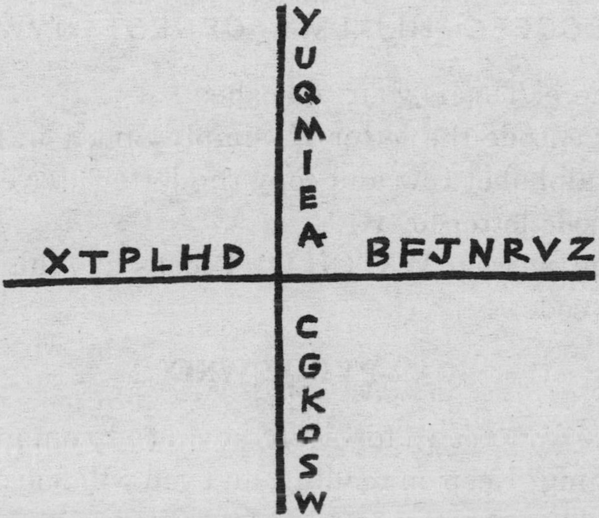

Reading from the outside edge to the center, each compass direction has a series of jumbled letters:

north = **YUQMIEA**
east = **ZVRNJFB**
south = **WSOKGC**
west = **XTPLHD**

Keep a list of the jumbled letters handy. You can use it to make any compass code message.

Try this for starters. Write all the letters in a row, beginning with north, then east, south, and west.

YUQMIEA ZVRNJFB WSOKGC XTPLHD

Below the row, write the letters of the alphabet.

YUQMIEA ZVRNJFB WSOKGC XTPLHD
ABCDEFG HIJKLMN OPQRST UVWXYZ

There! This is your code sheet.

To encode the letter **H**, simply find it in the bottom alphabet row and copy the letter above it. **Z** is the code letter for **H**.

The message **WATCH OUT** looks like this in compass code:

PYCQZ WXC

Are you ready for some advanced compass code training? Keep on reading, and you will learn how to befuddle even the smartest snoop.

Instead of writing the top row of letters in order of north, east, south, and west, mix up their arrangement. For example, make the order east, south, north, and west.

Then write down the alphabet below this new formation of letters.

ZVRNJFB WSOKGC YUQMIEA XTPLHD
ABCDEFG HIJKLM NOPQRST UVWXYZ

Now you have a new code sheet! This time, if you encode the message **WATCH OUT**, it will look completely different.

PZARW UXA ESNW

Can you guess what the last four letters mean? They don't form a word in your message. These letters are a clue for your friend so she knows how to unscramble your coded writing. They tell her the order of the jumbled letters in the top row.

ESNW means the top row of letters was written in the order of east, south, north, and west. **ESNW** stands for the first letter of each direction.

Here are more ways to scramble compass directions:

SENW

WNES

When your top row has these new groupings, the message **WATCH OUT** is coded as **PWAOV UXA SENW** or **OXBPU VWB WNES**.

There are 24 different ways to send the very same message in compass code. Amazing!

MYSTERY BOOK

Now try to figure out this book title:

FYBVYQ FYAII NESW

Did you get it? The book title is *Maniac Magee* by Jerry Spinelli.

The Shadow Code

One of the most clever codes ever invented first appeared in a detective story written in the 1930s. The hero who used the code was a mysterious man dressed in black named "The Shadow." He was featured in hundreds of crime-fighting adventures.

Here are the letters of the alphabet written in the shadow code:

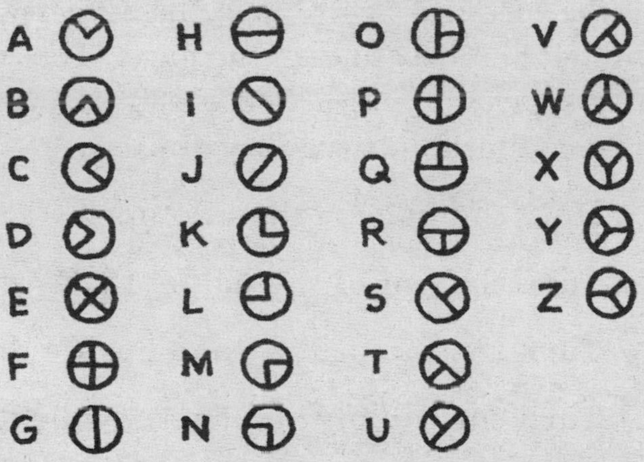

The shadow code is very unusual because most letters of the alphabet can be written in several ways. For example, here are four ways to encode the letter B:

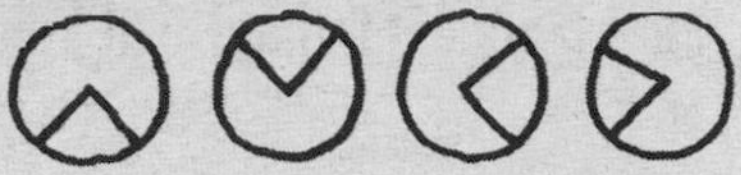

Can you see how this works? The first symbol is the usual way to write the letter. It looks like an upside-down V in a circle. The second symbol looks like the symbol for the letter A, but if you turn the page upside down, it becomes the symbol for B. (Try it and see.)

The third symbol looks like C, but if you turn the page partway to your right, it's the B symbol.

The fourth symbol looks like D, but if you turn the page partway to your left, it's B again.

Turning the page around to read the message is the secret behind the shadow code. But the person writing the message has to give the reader a clue that will tell him how to turn the page. The clue is a pointer symbol. There are four pointer symbols, one for each direction. Here they are:

 **Hold the page right-side up.**

 **Turn the top of the page to your right.**

 **Turn the top of the page upside down.**

 **Turn the top of the page to your left.**

To show you how the shadow code works, here is the message **SEND HELP FAST** written in two ways. First, without the pointer symbols:

Here is the same message written with pointers:

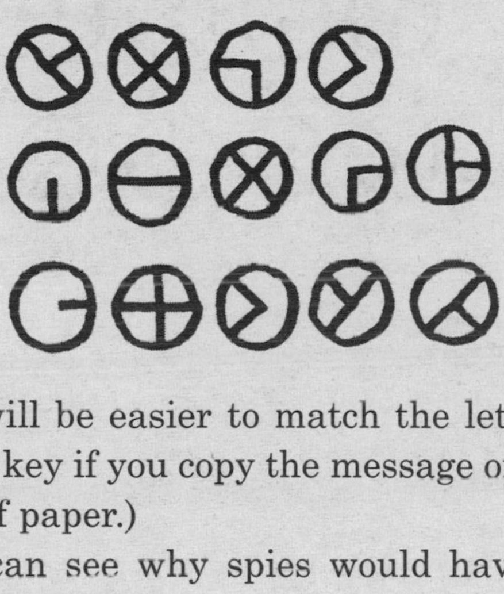

(Note: It will be easier to match the letters with the alphabet key if you copy the message onto a separate piece of paper.)

Now you can see why spies would have a hard time breaking this code. Even if they were to find the alphabet key, they might not think to turn the page.

Copy these symbols and use the shadow code to figure out the title of this adventure story. We have made it tougher to decode by breaking the title into groups of four symbols. (Watch for the pointers!)

If you decoded the title as Daniel Defoe's *Robinson Crusoe*, you have the "point" of the shadow code!

THE SNEAKY BUTTERFLY

Years before he founded the Boy Scouts, Robert Baden-Powell was an intelligence officer in the British army—and a resourceful one at that.

In the early 1890s, Baden-Powell was sent to spy on Kotor, an important naval base on the Adriatic Sea. His mission was to bring back a map of the fort there.

Baden-Powell knew that the guards would question anyone found near the fort, so he decided to disguise himself as a butterfly collector.

He climbed the hills of Kotor carrying butterfly nets and a sketchbook in which he had already drawn several butterflies. While making believe he was hunting insects, he scouted the area and sketched some very special butterflies.

When sentries stopped Baden-Powell, he was proud to show them his drawings. The guards didn't realize that some were clever maps. Carefully disguised marks on the butterflies' wings outlined the fortress and pinpointed the position and size of its guns. (We've made the map above easy to see. Baden-Powell's were well disguised.) Baden-Powell was free to return to his base with his hidden maps.

The Date Code

Quick! What is today's date?

If you are not sure, check it out. You will need it for sending secret messages using the date code.

Once you master this clever code, it will be tough for anyone to crack. It changes for each of the 365 days of the year (366 in a leap year).

Suppose today's date is February 4, 1999. Read on and you will discover how this date can scramble your confidential messages.

February is the second month of the year. So the date can be written as 2-4-99. If you remove the dashes, you have 2499.

To disguise the word **COWBOYS** using the date code, first write the date—as numbers—over the first four letters. Then keep repeating the digits over each of the next letters until you reach the end of the word. It will look like this:

2 4 9 9 2 4 9
C O W B O Y S

The number above each letter tells you how many places forward to shift in the alphabet. So, to code the word begin by moving forward two letters from the **C**. It becomes an **E**.

A B C D E F G H I J K L M N O P Q R...

Now to the next letter, **O**. Since the number 4 is above it, move ahead four letters in the alphabet. It becomes an **S**.

If a count advances past **Z**, go back to the beginning of the alphabet and keep counting. In this example, the **W** becomes an **F**.

When you finish, **COWBOYS** is coded as:

ESFKQCB

Nifty, isn't it? Notice that the letter **O** is coded as **S** the first time and as **Q** the second. That's what makes the date code hard to decipher.

Tip: If a zero is above a letter, don't count forward —it is coded as itself.

Now that you have the hang of it, try to mix up this message using the date code and February 4, 1999:

GREG HAS NO SOCKS ON

Did you work it out? Your coded message should read:

IVNP JEB WQ WXLMW XW

You can disguise your message to look like a note to a friend. Date it and sign your name. And to confuse a spy even more, break up the message using different spacing.

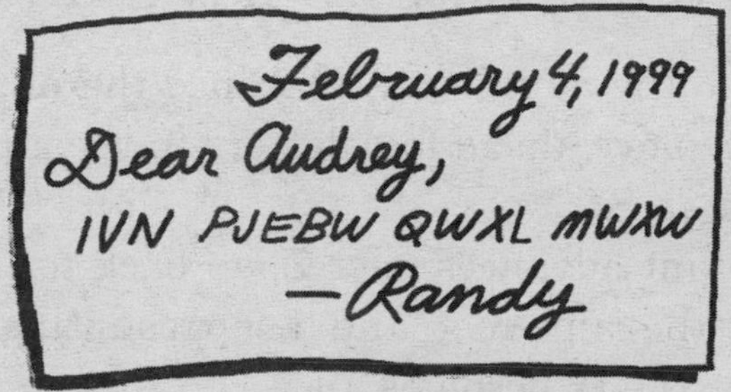

When your friend receives the note, first he glances at the date. Instantly he knows how to decode it. To start, he writes this date above your message.

249 92499 2499 2499
IVN PJEBW QWXL MWXW

Then he shifts *backward* in the alphabet the same number of places written above each letter. Your message quickly appears!

MYSTERY BOOK

Now it is your turn. Read the note below that encodes a first-rate book.

June 10, 1997
Dear Code Club Pal,
GXRR UQME RUZJMN
—Codemaster

The title is *A Wrinkle in Time* by Madeleine L'Engle.